I Miss You, Father Bear

BY ELSE HOLMELUND MINARIK

ILLUSTRATED BY CHRIS HAHNER

 HarperFestival®
A Division of HarperCollinsPublishers

Little Bear and Mother Bear were watching the sunset.
"I wish Father Bear would come home,"
said Little Bear. "I miss him!"

"I do too," said Mother Bear.
Little Bear asked, "When Father Bear is on his boat,
can he see the sunset?"

"Oh, yes," said Mother Bear,
"because Father Bear is a fisherman.
Fishermen must get up early and go to bed late.
Father Bear can see both the sunset and the sunrise."

Little Bear thought about what Mother Bear said.

He said, "I will see the sunrise tomorrow, just like Father Bear."

Mother Bear laughed, saying, "You don't get up that early, Little Bear."

"But tomorrow I will!" said Little Bear.

As Mother Bear read a story, Little Bear had an idea.
He told Mother Bear, "I'm not going to sleep.
I'll stay awake to see the sunrise—just like Father Bear.
Then I won't have to get up early!"

Mother Bear told Little Bear, "You are too little to
stay awake—but you can try it.
Anyway, here's a good night kiss."

"I can do it!" Little Bear said to himself.

"I can stay awake."

He opened his eyes wide. He tossed and turned.

He looked at the moonlight. And then he got up.

"Mother Bear," Little Bear called. "I am thirsty."

Mother Bear brought Little Bear a glass of water.
Little Bear asked, "How long until the sun comes up?"
"A whole night long," said Mother Bear.
"First the moon goes to bed, and then the sun wakes up."

"It's too hot in here," said Little Bear.
Mother Bear opened the window and said,
"Now go to sleep, Little Bear."

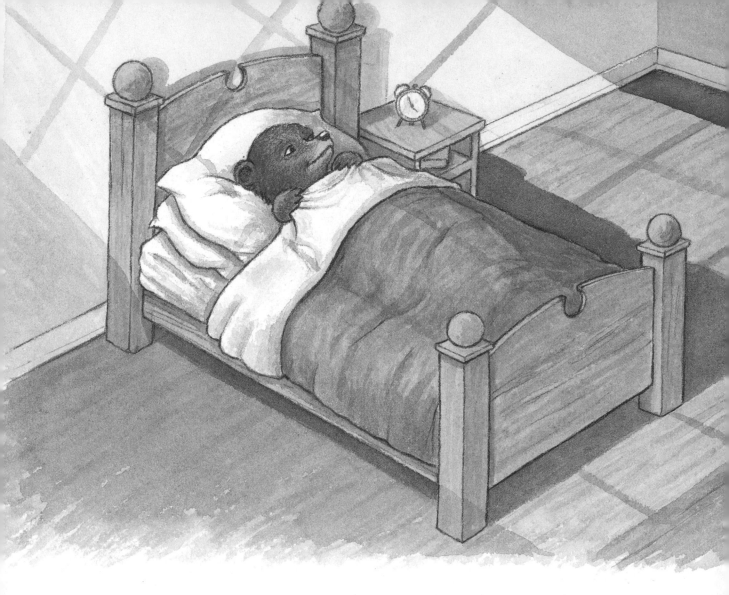

Little Bear lay down again and thought of Father Bear.
"I wonder what he is doing now?" said Little Bear.
"Is it too late to go fishing?"

"I know what," said Little Bear, "I'll go fishing, too!"
He slipped out of bed and went down the hall.
He got an umbrella from the rack,
and tiptoed quietly back to his room.

Little Bear made a fishing rod from the umbrella and a tie.
Then he could fish off the end of his bed.
And that's just what he did.

The sea was very rough, and the waves were very big.
Little Bear rocked back and forth on his boat—the bed.

There was a crash. Little Bear had fallen off the bed.
Mother Bear heard the noise. She came into the room.

Mother Bear was quite cross.
"Little Bear—what are you up to now?" she said.
"You should be asleep!"

Little Bear explained, "I was pretending to be Father Bear. It made me feel like I was with him. I miss him!"

"I know," said Mother Bear. She kissed him.
"But I think you should go to sleep now. When you wake up,
Father Bear will be even closer to coming home."
And so Little Bear slipped under his blankets.

Little Bear went to sleep.
There was a smile on his little face.
He was dreaming of Father Bear.

In the morning, Little Bear came down for breakfast.
Mother Bear gave him his oatmeal and said,
"I'm sorry you didn't see the sunrise, Little Bear."

"I didn't see the sunrise, but I did dream about Father Bear,"
said Little Bear happily.
"Oh," said Mother Bear, "so did I! That must mean
that Father Bear will soon be home again."

Little Bear ate his oatmeal as he looked out at the sea.
In between spoonfuls he smiled, because he knew
Father Bear would soon be coming home.